ALPHONSE, THAT IS NOT OK TO DO!

Daisy Hirst

WALKER BOOKS

AND SUBSIDIARIES

LONDON • BOSTON • SYDNEY • AUCKLAND

ONCE there was Natalie

and then, there was
Alphonse too.

Natalie mostly did not mind there being Alphonse.

They both liked naming the pigeons,

Banana!

Lorraine!

bouncing
things
off the
bunkbeds

and stories in
the chair,

and they both loved
making things.

Except that Alphonse did
sometimes draw on the
things that Natalie made,

or eat
them,
and
Natalie
hated
that.

One day when lunch was peas

and telly
was awful

and Mum did not understand,

Natalie found Alphonse under the bunkbeds ...

eating her favourite book.

"ALPHONSE, THAT IS NOT OK TO DO!" said Natalie.

Behind the big chair, Natalie drew ...

a tornado,

two beasts,

a swarm of peas

and Alphonse, very small.

but
Natalie
put her
fingers in
her ears
and went
for her
bath.

Outside the bathroom,
Natalie heard noises.
She thought she heard ...

a roaring tornado,

"Alphonse? Mum?" called Natalie.
"Alphonse, are you OK?"

It was very quiet.

Natalie opened
the door.

"Natalie, I only tried to get the sticky tape down," said Alphonse, "so I could fix your book.

Only I couldn't reach it, so I tried to suck it down with the hoover,

ROAR!

then I got the chair to stand on, but I sort of ran over the cat,

then I climbed up, but everything fell on my head and then so did the marbles."

"Are you hurt?" said Natalie.

"No," said Alphonse. "I'm sorry I ate your book."

"It's OK," said Natalie. "I'm sorry I was mean."

"I finished your picture," said Alphonse.

Natalie thought it was ...

Most Excellent
Fantastic!

So they had better
draw quite a few more.